The
Bells
of
Lake
Superior

For Eileen — all good wishes.

Dayton O. Hyde

Chautauqua
2001

The
Bells
of
Lake
Superior

by Dayton O. Hyde

Boyds Mills Press

Published by Caroline House
Boyds Mills Press, Inc.
A Highlights Company
815 Church Street
Honesdale, Pennsylvania 18431
Printed in the United States of America

Publisher Cataloging-in-Publication Data
Hyde, Dayton O.
     The bells of Lake Superior / by Dayton O. Hyde.—1st ed.
[104]p. :   cm.
Summary : A budding young composer, who earns money as a chimney
sweep, tunes the town's various church bells to harmonize and writes his
first symphony. In doing so, he sparks unity among the townspeople.
ISBN 1-56397-188-7
1. Composers—Juvenile literature—Fiction. [1. Composers—Fiction.] I. Title.
813.5 [F]—dc20   1995   CIP
Library of Congress Catalog Card Number 94-71022

First edition, 1995
Book designed by Tim Gillner
The text of this book is set in 12-point Palatino.

10 9 8 7 6 5 4 3 2

For Phyllis Rankin, librarian,
who gave a small boy a love of books and
risked her job to let him read
beyond his years

PROLOGUE
◆◆◆◆◆◆◆◆◆◆◆◆◆◆◆◆◆◆◆◆

The wind off Lake Superior blew cold tears into the old man's eyes. It was already late afternoon, and the slabs of the concrete bench were hard against his lean bottom. Despite his heavy wool trousers, he could feel the wintry chill seeping into his bones. A gray mist crept over the park, and even in his fur-lined gloves, his fingers were beginning to numb.

Kersplash! A big wet snowflake splashed down his pink forehead, hit a furrow in his cheek, and dribbled off his jowl. "Not snow!" he thought, shaking his head. The old man had come to his favorite spot to watch neighborhood kids zoom down the black ice of Cook's Hill on their homemade sleds. A wet snow would slow down the activity.

He glanced up fondly at the big bronze statue on the gray marble slab behind the bench and smiled to himself.

Most city parks displayed statues of famous generals long dead, mounted on tirelessly prancing horses; this huge sculpture paid tribute to a boy he knew and loved, someone who was very much alive.

The boy wore a tall stovepipe hat, and he was perched daringly on a bicycle, steering with one hand and holding a flute in the other. The bicycle had a great big front wheel, taller than the boy, and a tiny one, terrier high, in back. He rode on a little seat way up high, and tied to the bicycle were a chimney sweep's brushes and ropes—the tools of his trade.

The old man glanced across the park at the steep snowy roofs, church spires, and chimneys that seemed to keep the clouds at bay. Cleaning chimneys had been dangerous for the boy; he had climbed up there in all sorts of weather, even in wintertime with all that ice and snow. The old man remembered the first time he had seen the lad sailing from one roof to another on frozen ropes no bigger around than his thumb.

A wool bundle of a child, pulling his sister along on a little red sled, interrupted the man's reverie. The boy glanced up at him shyly. "Good evening, Professor Trombley," he said as the iron runners grated against a patch of bare sidewalk. "I'd stop to visit with you, but my sister wants to go home."

The old man watched as the boy, the girl, and the sled moved into the gathering darkness. He unbuttoned his heavy overcoat, fumbled for his watch chain, and pulled out his big, round pocket watch. It was three minutes to five, and soon the church bells across the park would begin summoning parishioners to an early evening service. He shivered uncontrollably, closed his coat, and worked at the buttons with stiffening fingers.

Kersplash! Another snowflake sloshed down the old man's face. The cheeks of the bronze boy above him were streaked as the wet snowflakes landed on the greenish patina of the metal and melted into tears. "Ah, my lad, you're missing us! I wish you were here tonight; it's pork chop night. With applesauce. If I'm not mistaken, your mother has prepared one of her deep-dish apple pies, and I'm invited for dinner."

He rose stiffly from the bench. It was beginning to snow heavily, and already the street lamps were wearing lopsided hats of snow. Time to say good-bye to the statue and go home. "Be seeing you, my lad," he muttered to the figure, and it seemed that the bronze boy wiggled his flute and winked an eye.

That night, as he lay snug and warm in the gables of his little house in the forest, the old man listened to the night wind making music in the creaking, frozen branches of the maple trees. Now the wind strummed amongst the eaves, and the murmur sounded like the chuckle of happy voices. So much had happened in this once solemn, unhappy town. He sighed and concentrated on relaxing his tired muscles, snuggling deep into his blankets. That boy!

There were just five days left of the old year. He hoped that 1898 would be a great year for the boy and for the town. As he drifted off, the old man thought he heard the music of a flute from somewhere on high. He went to sleep smiling, reliving events dear to his heart.

CHAPTER ONE

◆◆◆◆◆◆◆◆◆◆◆◆◆◆◆◆◆◆◆◆

It was the kind of night wind that blows uninvited down chimneys, scattering ashes on the hearths of rich and poor alike—the kind of brute force that startles sparrows from their roosts, sticks their feathers on backward, and flings them earthward to feed alley cats. It was savage enough to toll the bell in a belfry without a pull on the rope. As the constable's lantern swept the steep, icy spine of the church roof, the little chimney sweep snugged his bundle of brushes against his back, doubled the thin rope around his gloved hands, checked to see that it was still anchored to the corner post of the belfry, and kicked free.

As he swung into frozen darkness, the wind laughed at him, threatening to dash his slender body against the sandstone slabs of the bell tower. Kicking away from the wall, he pumped his legs. Once, twice, thrice, he swung out over the abyss between church and rectory. Then, as a circle of lantern light engulfed him like a pack of baying hounds, he grinned down at the frustrated constable and plunged like a dropped stone to a shadowed valley on the rectory roof, where wind had broomed the snow away.

After three taps on a curtained garret window, a chain of sounds commenced within. He heard the scrape of a chair on rough boards, mutterings of bother, then shuffling, slippered steps. The rattle of a latch came next, and the creak of hinges plagued with an arthritis of rust. Shrugging off his burden of brushes, the boy heaved them over the sill, summoned his last bit of strength, and slid after them into the blessed warmth of the tiny apartment.

The woman was already shuffling back to her chair. "Just once," she said. "Just once I'd like to have a son who comes in the front door like a normal child." She shook her graying head in despair, but then smiled faintly. "You're back off the rooftops though, Tommy. That's what matters, hey?"

The chair yelped a complaint as though she were sitting down on a puppy. "Well, what have you brought home this time? A leg of spring lamb? Some parsley and a tin of mint jelly? Hah! Don't I wish."

"I'd like some, too, Ma," the chimney sweep said. "But I couldn't find a speck of work; nobody would believe I'd go up on the roofs in this weather. All I brought is church cheese and spuds again. And tea. The label's gone, but the grocer swore it was good stuff."

The wind rattled the windows, and a cold draft blew out one of the candles. Above the buffeting of the storm came the uncertain, wobbly wail of the town's police sirens. The boy listened thoughtfully. "Close one tonight, Ma," he said. "You know that big old constable they call 'Moose'? The one who tried to arrest me for singing from the rooftops? Well, tonight I plumb forgot all about curfew. Crossing Main, I dropped a chimney brush and had to go back looking for it. The Moose was parked behind a carriage, watchin' for trouble, and he jumped his bicycle out after me. I scrammed it to the roofs. Nobody's going to follow me then, right? Should have seen the look on his face when I zoomed from the church to the rectory. Bet he thought he'd seen an angel!"

Tommy's mother sat with her face turned away from him, and he stopped talking suddenly to look at her.

"You've been cryin', Ma," he said. "I'll bet it was those church ladies again, talkin' about Pa. They sure know how to get your attention!"

The woman thumbed a spilled tear from her aproned knee. "They went to the board of vestrymen today and tried to get me fired from my job cleaning the church. Said I had no business living here on church property, what with a husband who died in prison. If we had to leave here, Tommy, I wouldn't know where to go! To another town? Where else could you study music with a man like the Professor?"

Tommy's jaw clenched in anger. "It's not us, Ma. Folks in this town hate each other like two cats in a sack. Listening to them talk—it's like hearing an orchestra where the violins, violas, and the piano are all out of tune." The boy flushed, as though confessing something he was ashamed of. "All day long when I work up there on those roofs, talk floats up the chimney to me. Bad stuff I'm not supposed to hear. People sayin' such hateful, hurtful things to each other. Then I pass 'em on the street, and they practically spit on me 'cause I sweep chimneys. Don't you take it on your shoulders, Ma. There's somethin' wrong with this town."

Tommy warmed his hands before the stove, working suppleness back into each finger. As his mother stood at the stove preparing supper, he reached for a battered black case on the floor and took out a silver flute. Caressing it lovingly, he put it to his lips and ran a scale, filling the room with quick, lively magic.

It was a fine instrument. Solo quality. His dad had been so sure of his talent that he'd stolen money from a drinking buddy to buy a flute of the best quality for his son. And he'd gotten caught.

"It was so sad!" Tommy thought. "Six months in prison! Six months making burlap bags in a jute mill. I could have played music on a hollow stick." With one month left to serve, Tommy's father had died in a mill accident.

For a long time afterward, the boy refused to touch the instrument. Then, one day, he took it out of its case, blew a note or two, and suddenly realized how much he had missed playing. He missed those Sunday concerts in the park, German band style, with lots of brass. His father had lived all week long to hear them. And now his son was back, playing in the band, writing music even. Some folks thought he was better than Beethoven, but Tommy knew better.

"Time to practice," he said suddenly. "What do you feel like hearing tonight, Ma? Beethoven? Some Brahms I heard on a player piano?"

She smiled at him wearily. "Anything, so long as it's happy," she said. "Tonight I could use a lift. Something lively and bright—something to help me quit thinking about our troubles."

CHAPTER TWO

♦♦♦♦♦♦♦♦♦♦♦♦♦♦♦♦♦♦♦♦♦♦

A rime of black ice from the night storm coated the rooftops as Tommy climbed out the window to begin his day. It was Sunday, and instead of being burdened with chimney-cleaning brushes, ropes for climbing, and canvas for gagging the mouths of fireplaces, he carried only the scuffed black case containing his precious flute.

Ahead of him, a skiff of fine powder snow hid a rink of ice on the steep of the roof. Suddenly he slipped and went down hard, caroming off the frame of a heavy glass skylight and skidding to the very brink of the abyss, where the toe of his boot caught on the metal gutter and held. Forty feet below him, he could see the cold, black, decorative spears of a wrought-iron fence waiting to impale him. Clinging for dear life, he managed to grasp a nearby vent pipe and pull himself away from danger. For a long moment he lay without moving, feeling his heart pound through aching ribs as though ready to burst.

"Wow! That was close! Quit dreaming, pal!" He got to his knees and beat the snow dust from his jacket. For a sweep his age, he had spent a lot of time on rooftops, roaming them in weather that would have sent tough men scurrying for cover. But careless sweeps had a way of dying young. He'd better mind his business.

From his vantage point, he could read the clock set in somber sandstone above the entrance of the Union Bank. It was almost eight o'clock. In a few moments, the Catholic church bells at the Irish end of town would start having a horrible dogfight with the Episcopal bells overhead, joined by those of the Methodists on the hill and a cacophony from both Lutherans and Presbyterian down by the lake. The churches fought doglike for a congregation, as though each wayward soul were a soup bone.

Gifted with faultless pitch, Tommy hated that discord with a passion. When the bells quarreled, his head pounded, and his first impulse was to run as far away from the sound as possible.

Bong! Bong! Bong! went the Episcopal bells suddenly, getting a head start on the others.

Blang! Blang! Blang! went the Methodists, trying to catch up.

Whang! boomed the Catholics. *Whang! Whang! Whang!*

Tinkle! Tinkle! Tinkle! went the Lutherans, playing a little bell tune left over from Christmas.

Thunk! Thunk! Thunk! went the Presbyterian bell, around whose clapper the night wind had knotted the bell rope.

Tommy lay with his jacket pulled up over his ears until every last peal had blown out over Lake Superior on the prevailing wind. His skull pounded with remnants of that savage disharmony. Man's music at its worst!

But new sounds, comfortable and familiar, floated up to him and kept forming in his head, part of a symphony he felt deeply but as yet had not enough confidence to write. Listening intently, he could hear percussion instruments in the *clippity-clop, clippity-clop, clop-clippity* of the hooves of Mr. Stinglein's horse delivering the last of the morning's milk up on Arch Street.

From a great, gaunt sugar maple came nervous chirpings, a rowdy chattering of wintering sparrows that had fled the bell towers. High above, Tommy heard sudden cries, like a bassoon with a defective reed, as a flock of herring gulls circled overhead on their way from some frozen dumpling of an iceberg on Lake Superior to breakfast at the city dump south of town.

Moving carefully across a series of connected roofs and taking care not to send an avalanche of snow down over the eaves as he passed, Tommy hummed an aria from *Rigoletto*. Now and then he would cease his music to listen down a chimney here and a chimney there, as though to determine whether the inhabitants of the house had survived the competition of those awful church bells. At last he reached his destination and settled himself on the chimney cap of a large, ornate brownstone dwelling, where a welcome thermal of warm air rose from an inefficiency of fireplaces within.

The mansion belonged to John Branch, a strange, blustery man who had his fingers in most of the financial pies in town. He was a man who hated music, hated art, and hated games. He seldom spoke to those not within his immediate circle of pompous fools—except to refuse a loan, or to mouth platitudes about the virtues of hard work, even though he had a big staff to do his own.

Along the distant railroad tracks an engineer, high and safe in the cab of his steam locomotive, sounded his lonely whistle at a crossing to warn all horses and wagons in the area that the train was about to come roaring through. Tommy could hear far-off rumblings as the train came down the grade, setting dogs to barking and chickens to cackling, and waking the Sunday sleepers in the village beyond the hill.

Sitting cross-legged on the bare chimney cap, he warmed his fingers for a moment in the welcome heat, then took his slender flute from the case. It too was cold and stiff, and he held it for a few minutes in the warm thermal. The finger mechanism slowly relaxed. Tommy played a soft warm-up scale. From a giant American elm in the front yard, a puffed-up robin, either the last one of autumn or the first of spring, perked up at the music, smoothed the trapped air out of its feathers, and joined with a querulous plea for rain.

"Ladies and gentlemen," Tommy announced to the robin and a scolding blue jay, "Sir Tommy Parkman will now play an arrangement for the flute written especially for him by his friend Mozart, and entitled *The Magic Flute.*"

Bowing solemnly to the two birds, the boy listened thoughtfully as though to some invisible orchestra, then, nodding his head to establish the beat, raised his flute and began to play.

Swaying gently back and forth, bracing against a north wind that came playfully to nip at the sleeves of his thin cotton jacket and to blow whole measures of notes away, the boy gave his heart to the world below. The sweet purity of his tones flowed down into the massive flue of the chimney and out through the fireplaces, flooding the sober rooms of the house with musical passages like errant sunbeams.

Excitement danced like fireflies in Tommy's eyes as he heard faint stirrings deep within the house. "Maybe it's Betsy!" he thought. He pictured Branch's tall, pretty daughter sitting up suddenly in bed and shaking blonde curls from her face. Thrilling to his music, and rubbing her eyes as though they were magic lamps that could bring the musician to her side.

Betsy the Unobtainable! She was to Tommy the most beautiful girl in the world. How often, hidden behind a chimney on a rooftop far above her head, had he watched as some oaf carried her books home from school? How often had he played his heart out to her as she peered up through a leafy bower in the trees, searching for the source of the trills as though expecting a nightingale?

At school he was just a face in the chattering crowd. In his mind he dared long conversations with her about music, but in reality he could not even manage a friendly smile as they passed in the halls. He could have met her at school events, but he had little time for anything that vied with his music. With the clang of the final bell each day, he rushed off—either to practice his music with Professor Trombley or to augment his mother's slender income by sweeping chimneys.

Hearing the music that stole uninvited into his house, John Branch leapt out of his seat at the breakfast table with such violence that he sent dishes to the floor and smashed a porcelain sugar bowl that had managed to survive thirty years of domestic disharmony.

"Betsy!" he roared. "How many times have I told you? No music until I've left this house, do you hear?"

Unaware of the havoc he was creating, Tommy fingered a happy cluster of sweet little notes. Eyes closed in rapture, he was a tiny goldfinch, perched jauntily on the branch of some ancient maple, singing to a mate on the nest.

John Branch's neck went from spring beauty to wild rose, then from blackberry to black cherry. "Betsy! Do you hear me? That music gives me a headache! First it was those damned church bells this morning, now it's a blasted Gramophone. Stop it right now!"

"I can't stop, Father!" she protested from the stairway. "I can't stop because I'm not playing any music. Maybe it's coming from the neighbor's house."

Tommy ceased playing as the front door shot open, then slammed angrily behind John Branch himself. "Stop that infernal racket!" he shouted to the world, looking right and left over the deserted lawns and cold iron fences. Seeing no one and hearing nothing, he shook his fist at the only possible offender, the heavens, and stormed back into the house.

Tommy chuckled, raised himself back on his ledge, and warmed his fingers for a moment. "That old grouch! How does Betsy manage to put up with him?" Through the chimney flue, he could hear the man cranking angrily away at a telephone.

Tommy played only a few more bars of music before he heard the siren start on the police wagon. At first, it sounded more like the threatening growl of a dog getting ready to bite the postman, then it began to squeal as though the grease in the howler were cold. Finally, it built to a high, wailing scream like a soprano with a mouse in her stocking. There was the far-off rumble of iron wheels on cobblestones and shod hooves striking against rock. Tommy slipped off his perch just as John Branch stepped out the front door to wait for the police wagon.

Quietly, the boy stowed his flute in its case and eased the snaps shut, carefully mapping out his escape route. He would have to wade across a powdery field of newly drifted snow just above the banker's head, cut up over the roof cap, and slide down to the bottom of the north slope, where it was an easy leap to the roof of the carriage house. From there, he could descend to the neighbor's fence by way of a spindly old spruce, then hit a long, sloping roof that would take him high again to safety.

Silent as a wolf, he moved unnoticed across the drift and had almost reached the top of the steep roof when the whole snowfield began to move beneath him.

"Look out!" he shouted to the enemy below, but it was too late. With a thunderous roar, the avalanche swept Tommy over the eaves, entombing the boy and Betsy's father in a mountain of white.

For a moment, Tommy's legs seemed anchored in the soft mass. The pile of snow on his left began to move, assuming the identity of a sputtering, angry man. John Branch's eyes were just beginning to blink free when Tommy hurled a fresh cloud of snow into the man's face and took off. By the time the police arrived to help the fuming banker out of the drift, they found little more of Tommy than bootprints in the snow.

CHAPTER THREE

◆◆◆◆◆◆◆◆◆◆◆◆◆◆◆◆◆◆◆◆

Professor Trombley leaned back, daring the balance point of his hard oak chair as he listened to Tommy practice. A big tear rolled down one pink, wrinkled cheek and escaped into his white rat of a moustache. He sat with his eyes closed tightly, as though to dam the flood waters of his emotions. He drummed the beat softly on his protruding tummy with his wrinkled but still elegant violinist's fingers.

Besides a few pots and pans, an old cot, and a Confederate gray, government-issue blanket, there was little in the room not associated with music. There were a half dozen decrepit music stands awaiting the local musicians who dropped by for an evening of chamber music, a metronome, and untidy stacks of frazzled, handwritten sheet music. The dust that covered it all could be forgiven the old man because of his fading eyesight.

Yellowed newspaper clippings, stuck carelessly to the wall with common pins, showed that the Professor cared little for past fame. Only by reading the playbills would you know that the man was on the downside of a once-illustrious career that had spanned half a century.

Never one to think of himself, the old musician had given his savings to an ailing friend, holding out just enough to buy a one-way ticket to northern Michigan, where he had been invited to live out his years with a daughter who owned a business and was "doing very well."

Through no fault of his, it hadn't worked out. "Here I am, my boy, teaching music for a few pennies," he told Tommy. "But it's worth it, lad, just to hear you play. When you are having one of your good days, you show greatness, and that's a compliment from a man who never passes words lightly from his lips."

But now, as Tommy lost his concentration and stumbled over an easy passage, the Professor rocked forward on his chair, slamming the front legs down hard on the floor. "Enough!" he cried. "Already your fingers are becoming stiff like mine! You do nothing to protect yourself! Every day after school you rush to the roof-tops and it's work, work, work, high in the cold winds, cleaning chimneys. I tell you what, boy. I will sell my Stradivarius violin and send you off to music school. They will soon know you for a rare genius!"

Tommy looked at the old man, trying to mask the sadness he felt. "Professor Trombley, you've already..."

"Use my name, lad, to get an audition. Once they've heard you, Tommy boy, they'll get excited. No end of scholarships for a major talent like you. I'll go down to the newspaper office and talk to advertising. We'll put an ad in for that old fiddle. Worth ten thousand if it's worth a silver dollar! We could use that money now, couldn't we?"

"Professor Trombley, you sold your violin last year," Tommy said, but the old man was excited and did not seem to hear.

"I want you to stop cleaning chimneys immediately," the Maestro ordered. "Too dangerous. Too hard on your body. You might get your fingers pinched in the rope! What's a flutist without fingers, Tommy? What indeed?"

The old man cradled a mug of hot tea in his hands, enjoying the warmth. "But maybe that would be a good thing. Then you would have to be a composer. You have what it takes to write beautiful music. It is in here, boy," he said, patting his chest. "But first you must study, study, study. Sometimes I despair about you. You never seem to come down off the rooftops except for school."

Tommy smiled. "I guess that's true. I like it up there. It's sort of like owning your own private mountain range. The sounds of this old town rise up around me like a symphony just begging to be composed." His face flushed deeply with emotion. "I'll do it someday, Professor. Honest I will! I won't let you down! My symphony will have church bells, wagon rumbles, foghorns, storm winds, the rattle of sleet on tin, bird songs, people's anger, children's laughter, barking dogs, everything I hear from the rooftops. The music of this city will live forever, like Mozart's!"

Tears streamed down both of their faces. "I know you will do it, Tommy," the Professor said, turning his wrinkled face away and dusting the blistered paint of the windowsill with his faded blue kerchief. "And believe me, I'll be proud!"

Sadness washed over the old man's face as he stood staring out the window. "Yes," he said. "Yes, the violin's gone, isn't it? I kept the case hanging there on the wall, pretending it still held my friend's body, my precious violin. I made some fine music with that one, but I had to let it go. It wasn't fair to the world to have that beautiful instrument remain silent."

The old man straightened the faded curtain. "When I think of what I've given away! I could have sent you to the finest music school with plenty to spare. And do you know what that scoundrel, John Branch, did to my daughter? When she got sick and had trouble paying her bills, he went around to all her creditors and got everyone to forgive her obligations. They did it gladly, of course; she had many friends. And after Branch talked everyone into writing off her debts, he foreclosed on her business. She died of a broken heart. I get furious every time I think of it!"

Tommy had heard the Professor's sad tale many times before, but now he pictured the old banker as he rose, sputtering, from the snowdrift. He chuckled to himself thinking about it, but then reality set in. In this town, it wouldn't do to have John Branch as an enemy.

CHAPTER FOUR

◆◆◆◆◆◆◆◆◆◆◆◆◆◆◆◆◆◆◆◆

Tommy cut across the elementary school roof, slid down a drainpipe, crossed an alley behind the grocery store, then went up high again, as though walking on the ground made him insecure. He paused to make snow angels in a huge white drift that had been driven by wind against the dome of the public library. Falling back repeatedly against the drift with arms spread wide, he left his likeness in the snow. Chuckling, he stood back to inspect his work. From the street, it might look like the work of some famous sculptor. He ducked out of sight when a well-dressed lady stopped her buggy and braved the cold long enough to admire his endeavors.

Digging in a drift atop the library, he recovered a rope he had cached there as part of his travel network. Knocking the ice off the strands, he checked the knots for tightness, then used the rope to sail across to an old fur trader's house that, although suffering from neglect, still set a standard for style amongst its neighbors.

For a few moments he leaned against the chimney, listening. Then, hearing nothing, he called down into the silence. "Hey, Mrs. Haskall! You OK? It's Tommy Parkman, your favorite chimney sweep!"

A few tiny balls of sleet ticked against the blackened tin chimney cap, but there were no other sounds. As he was about to leave, he heard a faint voice call his name.

"Tommy? Tommy!"

"Hey, I'm glad you answered, Mrs. Haskall," Tommy said, looking as if he were talking to the chimney. "I was some worried."

"I've fallen. Get me help. I can't reach the windows to signal anyone, and you can't get in. The door's locked."

"You just lie right there, ma'am! I'll send help just as soon as I can get down off this roof. And I'll get my ma to come over and help you for a few days."

"Bless you, boy!" There was silence again, then he heard her thin little voice. "Tommy? You won't let them take me away from my house, will you?"

"You got me on your side, Mrs. Haskall. I promise." A horse and buggy were coming down the street, and Tommy waited patiently as the driver stopped at the cross streets. He was wasting valuable time, but signaling the man was his best shot at getting immediate help. As he waited, he looked down from the rooftops, noticing for the first time what made this house stand alone amidst its more pretentious neighbors. Pride! He saw for the first time the gardens just emerging from the snows, the lovely statuary still wearing hats of ice. Someone cared for this place. You knew just by looking at it that families had grown up here and loved each other, and that children's laughter had filled the gardens, lawns, and porches.

Tommy had been so troubled about his symphony. It existed in his head and his heart, all right, but in so many fragmented pieces that he didn't know how to pull them all together. One of these days, it would all come like a dawning, and he knew this house and its garden would be part of his inspiration. Maybe there were gardens in all the yards and in all the hearts of this miserable town, just waiting to grow.

The horse and buggy were half a block away when Tommy began waving his arms frantically. The driver pulled up on his lines and watched as Tommy eased himself down to the edge of the roof nearest the street. But the man took out his pocket watch and pointed to it, indicating that he was too busy to stay longer. Then he drove away.

Tommy threw a rope around the chimney of the neighboring house and swung over easily, landing on a lower roof in a puff of snow. A woman had opened her dormer window and was leaning out, cleaning ice from the sill.

"Mrs. Casper!" he said, peering down over the eaves. "It's Tommy Parkman, the chimney sweep. Mrs. Haskall's fallen down, and she can't get help. Would you send word to a constable?"

The woman looked at him coldly. "What are you doing

on my roof? We don't want our chimneys cleaned!"

"I know," Tommy said. "I'm trying to get help for Mrs. Haskall. She's fallen."

"Serves her right," Mrs. Casper snapped. "Living there alone like that. Just causes no end of trouble for us neighbors. You'll have to find someone else to get the constable. I did it last time she fell, and a lot of good it did me."

Tommy shrugged and leaped to the next roof. Standing as close as he dared to the eaves, he called down to a big man in a red wool cap, who was unloading groceries from a buckboard.

"Mr. Wicks, sir! It's Tommy. Remember? I cleaned your flue after you had the fire scare. Mrs. Haskall, that nice old lady two doors down from you, she's fallen and can't get help. Would you get the constable, please?"

"Get him yourself!" the man snapped. "It's my day off, and my time's my own." He hurried up his front steps with a box of groceries and kicked open the door to his house.

"I'm scared she'll die!" Tommy called out, but the slamming of the door put an end to his entreaty.

It was a long, scary leap from the edge of the roof to the drift below, but Tommy decided to try it. He seemed to fall forever, and as he hit the ground, he twisted one ankle. Pain shot through his leg.

There was no stopping now, however. Limping, he crossed the icy street, dodging carriages that refused to slow down.

By the time he reached the city jail, his feet felt like hard lumps. A deputy constable he'd never seen before looked at him suspiciously as he stuck his head in the door.

"Old Mrs. Haskall over on Ridge," he said. "She's fallen. Just wants to be helped on her feet, but her front door is locked."

A half hour later, from a vantage point on the roof-tops, Tommy heard the creak of a wagon and the curses of an angry driver as the horses pulled up the hill to the old house.

"What an awful thing," he thought. "What an awful thing to be old and helpless in a town where nobody cares."

CHAPTER FIVE

◆◆◆◆◆◆◆◆◆◆◆◆◆◆◆◆◆◆◆◆◆

By noon, the late winter sunshine had caused gushes of sooty meltwater to overflow the gutters on the eaves. The church crowd, homeward bound, drifted more slowly than usual, picking their uncertain way along the slushy walks. To Tommy, even the faint suspicion of spring was a time for rejoicing.

He lay back against a bare, sun-warmed patch of dark gray shingles and let the heat soak through his jacket. Above him, black on a field of faultless azure, the first crow of the year flapped lazily, looking down first to the right, then to the left, for a chance to do some earthly mischief. Tommy lost the bird in the sun and looked down quickly to rest his watering eyes.

For a moment, he contemplated the folks down there on the street. He was in full view of them, but no one looked up. Instead, they stared gloomily at the sidewalk, as though the next step might catch them unaware and take them right off the edge of the world.

"They need to laugh," Tommy thought. "They need music to bring joy into their lives!"

Watching from on high, Tommy could see how each family group stayed within its own space. And yet some vague need for each other, as humans, held them loosely together.

"On a day like this, why isn't everyone happy?" Tommy mused. He watched the clusters of children, each dressed in somber, winter grays like so many fat little oysters in an ocean bed, and wondered why they weren't playing. If he were in their place, he'd be sailing matchstick boats down the gutter, playing marbles wherever the sun had bared a patch of lawn, or sticking jackknives into the sod in a game of mumblety-peg. The boy got up and stretched lazily, singing to himself.

"Down on the millpond sat some bullfrogs in the middle.
One played the flute and another played a fiddle.
One set the rhythm with a big bass drum,
While a singer sang deep with a chug-a-rum."

Tommy took his flute and moved to a flat black roof already steaming in the sunshine, where the tall chimneys of an apartment complex formed a perfect acoustical backdrop for his flute. Here was a tiny amphitheater the architects never dreamed they were creating. Here he could sing or play his heart out, yet even though the music spread over the park below, he was hidden from view. The sounds, reverberating off rough stones, were so elusive that no one could pinpoint the source.

For a few moments more, Tommy watched the people, wondering at the gloom that hovered over them like a gray shroud of gnats. When he began to play a bright little fugue, the mood seemed to lift. Suddenly people straightened their shoulders and walked with their heads a little higher.

But then the church bells tolled for the next service, and the mood was gone. Tommy covered his ears against their dissonance. The crowd surged forward as if trying to escape the brutal din, and family groups changed directions without warning. People bumped into each other as though they were suddenly disoriented. When a fist fight broke out between two men, nobody tried to break it up.

The bells stopped at last, but the men fought on. Tommy took up his flute and began to play. When next he looked at the crowd, they were laughing, and the fighters were shaking hands.

"It's magic!" Tommy whispered. "I can control them with my music. Some day I'm going to make this whole town happy again!" He launched into a classic love song from *Rigoletto,* and smiled to himself as couples suddenly walked shoulder to shoulder and children ran ahead to play. He was finishing an aria when he stopped abruptly. There, in the middle of the street, pressing her long coat to her slender body, stood Betsy.

She was looking at the building next door, where a brick wall echoed his notes. Then she seemed suddenly to locate the true source of the music and walked rapidly toward him, climbing some steep steps so that the chimneys no longer gave him cover. He was trapped, but he began to play again. When next he dared peek, she had withdrawn a hand from her pocket and was holding it like a white butterfly behind her ear. He had never seen her look more beautiful.

But as the girl came toward him once more, Tommy panicked. Rushing off across the rooftops, he slipped and slid, almost dropping his flute, taking chances he had never taken before. He sought one favorite hiding place, then another, but there was no peace to be found in any of them.

He was upset, but he had no idea why. What made him so shy around Betsy? He'd talked to lots of girls in his life. Well, maybe not *lots,* but some. Now he wished he had the moment to live over again. Why, he'd just smile at Betsy and say, "Hello, I'm Tommy Parkman. I clean chimneys, but I'm really studying to be a musician. It's nice to meet you. And I'm sorry I buried your father in a snowdrift. Do you think he'll ever forgive me?"

It would've been so easy! But now what? Tomorrow was a school day, and sooner or later he'd have to pass her in the hall. Why did she have to be so pretty, and why was he so afraid of meeting her?

For a time, he sat in the belfry of the Episcopal church and listened to the organist. That man had a love of Brahms. Tommy found the music soothing, but it did nothing to ease his troubles. Should he talk to his ma about girls? Nah. She'd only tell him he was too good for Betsy.

What about Professor Trombley? He'd seen the world,

the Professor had, and maybe he knew about girls and what to say to them. Tommy decided he'd go over to the musician's little house and fish around for some advice without letting the Professor know he even cared. Trouble was, the old man could see through his ruses and might cut right to the heart of things. "Take charge, my boy. Faint heart ne'er won fair lady."

What little courage Tommy could muster came from the fact that Betsy seemed to be trying to meet him. But why? Maybe she liked him! For an hour he sat hunched up on a wall overlooking the booming ice fields on the lake, then gave in to the cold.

As he approached the Professor's cottage, Tommy suddenly stopped short. There was Betsy, coming out the door. He ducked behind a patch of willows. Betsy paused on the front porch, turned and shook hands with the old man, then left and crossed the railroad tracks toward her end of town.

When she was out of sight, Tommy rushed in to see the Professor. "She came here!" he cried excitedly.

"Who?" the old man asked.

"Why, Betsy Branch! She goes to my school." He felt blood rush to his cheeks. "Did she want to talk about me?"

Bemused, the Professor looked at the boy. "Why, no. Not much, at least. Apparently, she has been trying to catch up with you to find out my address, but she said you always run away. This afternoon she gave up and tracked me down herself. Wants to take music lessons from me; she's going to major in music at Normal. I turned her down, of course. Said I was too busy."

Tommy sank to his knees in the middle of the room and pounded the floor with his fists. "How could you tell her that? I wanted to meet her! Why, you could have taught her piano, and I could have used her in concerts when she got good enough to accompany me!"

Professor Trombley smiled. "I did you a favor, my boy. It is the broken heart that writes the finest music!"

Tommy bristled and went stalking off. "The way *you* work it, Professor," he said, pausing at the door, "I'll never get close enough to her to get a broken heart."

CHAPTER SIX

◆◆◆◆◆◆◆◆◆◆◆◆◆◆◆◆◆◆◆◆

That night a wild snowstorm blew in off Lake Superior, dispelling all hope for an early spring. The town lay huddled and helpless against the merciless onslaught of the winds and the twenty-foot drifts that had soon accumulated.

Frustrated by the storm, Tommy sat in the apartment, mending a tear in a canvas tarpaulin. He used tiny stitches, trying to make the patch tight enough to turn back the smallest particle of soot coming down a chimney, thus avoiding the wrath of his housewife customers.

He tried to keep his mind off Betsy Branch. If only the Maestro had decided to give her lessons, it would have been a simple matter to get conversations started. By now, some other music teacher had probably signed her up for lessons.

Tommy made a mistake, ripped off the patch and started over, then threw down the canvas in exasperation. Concentration was impossible. "Maybe Ma will finish it," he thought.

Tommy began pacing the floor, imagining the worst. He pictured the girl striding up the front steps of the Branch's big house. "Father! You know that boy who was up on our roof and dumped snow all over you? I know who he is! He goes to my school and sweeps chimneys around town. Lives with his mother in the old rectory next to St. Luke's."

How often his mother had warned him. "Don't make waves, Tommy, or we'll be thrown out of here! Just do your chimneys, study hard, and practice your music. Maybe this town will forget about your pa and let us live in peace."

The boy heard a sound through the thin walls and stiffened. Maybe it was Father Livermore coming up the stairs, huffing and puffing with lung complaint and climbing up to give them their eviction notice.

He braced himself for the knock, but none came. Instead, he heard the slapping of the bell rope against the inner wall of the tower as someone far below began pulling the rope to summon the faithful for Communion. It would be a wasted effort, for who would come out in a storm like this one? Tommy buried his head in his arms, bracing himself against the clamor as the bells tolled. Vibrations shook the apartment. A water glass fell off the sink and shattered on the wooden floor.

When the bells had ceased, Tommy swept up the shards of glass and threw them into the garbage. He glanced in at his mother, but she had been ill of late, and slept the sleep of the exhausted.

The storm buffeted the windowpanes, and drifting snow so shut out the light that he could not see to read. Putting on his jacket, he tied the earflaps of his cap beneath his chin, took his flute, and let himself out the window.

The jagged rooftops did little to break the force of the wind. Fearful of avalanches, the boy waded hip-deep across a snow-filled trough, then sought flatter surfaces where the gales had exposed the slates.

Fighting for each breath, he tried to find his escape rope to the church roof, but it was buried. Because the buildings were close together, he could jump the gaps and move quickly across the rooftops. But now, in the storm, he had to play it safe, crossing only where it was easy—and that often meant going out of his way. He moved as slowly as a hundred-year-old man, ever ready to drop to his knees whenever the wind tried to pick him up and hurl him away.

He paused at a chimney to warm his hands. Voices, coming up the flue from the rooms below, outshrieked the winds. The Carlsons were fighting about money again. The storm had kept Mr. Carlson from going to work and trapped him into spending a whole day with his wife. Already they had cabin fever. Depressed by what he heard, Tommy moved away.

Below him, at street level, he heard a door slam. Old Man Moore came out, bundled in mackinaw and scarf, digging with a shovel in the snow for his newspaper.

"How's he going to find one little newspaper in such

a big drift?" Tommy wondered.

Finding nothing, the man muttered curses at the newsboy for not delivering and stormed back into his house.

Bullets of sleet stung Tommy's cheeks as he finally gained the church roof and headed over a bare patch of slate ruled by a violence of crosswinds. He was halfway across when the gale slapped him down, bruising one hip. It forced him to crawl until he reached the base of the bell tower. Scaling a ledge, he pulled himself in over the line of cold, silent bells, knocking a rime of ice onto the wooden floor below. Then, climbing a short ladder, he pushed up a trap door with the top of his head and squeezed through the hole into a tiny room hidden under the very cone of the tower roof.

This was his own special hiding place atop the world, a sanctuary where he kept his treasures, practiced his flute, and worked at writing his symphony.

Years back, the room had housed a set of carillon bells, but when the bells needed maintenance and there was no one closer than Chicago who knew how to fix them, the instruments remained silent and forgotten. In time the leather straps grew brittle with disuse and fell away.

For a time, when Tommy's father was having his troubles, the boy had hidden him here, but the man got restless and turned himself in. The boy had stuffed the inside of the louvered shutters with rags, set up a tiny stove, carried a small bench and table up piece by piece, brought in kerosene lamps, and made a place for himself. Coal for the stove he found in abundance along the railroad tracks, where it had fallen from the cars. He ventilated the stove with a length of piping stuck out through the roof.

His mother was a stickler for neatness, but here Tommy could relax. Dozens of sheets of handwritten music lay scattered like fallen leaves across the table, and only Tommy could have put them in any semblance of order.

Once out of the storm, he sat back to rest, let the cold seep from his bones, and waited for the shivering to stop. His head was filled with the random rhythms of the storm and discordant mutterings that were just what he happened to need for the end of the third movement.

At first he kept his gloves on as he penciled in the notes, but soon the sides of the little coal stove glowed cherry red, and the room became cozy warm.

Tommy listened to the howling of the wind dogs that were holding him at bay and tried to capture the same excitement in music. The wind thumped the clapboard like a muffled drumbeat. The hinges of the shutters squeaked like badly played violins. In the mournful howling about the eaves, he heard a bank of French horns.

Outside the tower, a loose board on the sill creaked like the mewing of a lost kitten. He felt another flow of music coming! The savagery of the storm made all the little angers of the townspeople seem small and foolish.

Tommy worried for a moment when the tower shuddered under a fresh onslaught, then lost himself in his work as a new energy moved through him. "You have the confidence of the ignorant," the Maestro would have said. But in spite of his age, he was a composer now, and the notes flowed as fast and furious as the storm winds could carry them. Forget what he didn't know. Forget that he was only thirteen and without much training. Tommy had natural instincts and talents that welled forth, spurred on by the depth of his feelings for the land and by his concern for the town and its people. His very shyness had kept him high on those rooftops, listening to the town from afar. Yes, that was it! The townspeople were singing through him, getting their one chance to vent their frustrations, their hopes, their joys, and their dreams in music.

Sometimes, as Tommy finished a page and scanned it, he threw it down on the floor in frustration and began again. But mostly the notes poured from his pencil, and he raced desperately, trying to keep up with the musical voices that filled his head.

Suddenly, as he reeled from exhaustion, he was aware that the storm had stopped. Only the faintest rumbles of disharmony came from the retreating banks of clouds on the horizon. Above his head was a spectacle of blue sky, fresh-laundered and clean, with all the tiny, irritating soot and dust particles broomed away by the wind.

"Yes," Tommy thought. "This is what my next movement should show. A fresh new start for the town! People waking after a storm, refreshed and reborn, with all their petty angers gone and their minds as clean as a new snow."

He took up another batch of paper and a fresh, sharp pencil, and began again. After the anger and discord of the first movement, here was a new beginning. Tranquility came suddenly—relief that the worst of life's storm was over—then the tiniest dawning, the birth of new hope, new gentleness, a new resolve in the hearts of the people.

Darkness stole in, but still Tommy wrote. His mother would worry if he didn't come home for supper, but he had to keep going. The lanterns in the town's windows flickered and went out, one by one. Stars appeared, and the faintest hint of the aurora borealis burned in the north. These were the lights of a distant city, some local folks said, reflected in the sky.

By the time dawn came, Tommy had fallen asleep in exhaustion, his forehead pressed against the final sheet of the second movement of Tommy Parkman's First Symphony.

CHAPTER SEVEN

◆◆◆◆◆◆◆◆◆◆◆◆◆◆◆◆◆◆◆◆

It has been said that the fire started in a shack along the railroad tracks, where some hobos were toughing out the storm. Had the fire wagons been able to operate, the blaze would have been put out quickly. As it was, the wagons made it to the first heavy snowdrifts and no farther, so the fire began leaping from one shack to another.

"Good riddance of bad rubbish," John Branch chortled, mouthing one of his favorite platitudes. Looking down from his house on the hill over an ocean of dirty, black smoke, he smiled to himself. "I hope it takes the next ten blocks," he muttered. "For years, I've been trying to pick up that land for factories. Now the riffraff will be forced to sell out cheap! Wait till they find out I own the mortgage on every last building! Think of it! After the fire, they'll be glad enough to have someone with money come in and clean up that mess!"

Tommy saw the holocaust from his room in the church tower, watching helplessly as the first fire wagon slammed into a drift and stuck. The eight big draft horses strained against their harnesses. Their steel shoes struck sparks on the pavement, but the wagon wouldn't budge. The fire was headed straight down the row of old shacks and warehouses toward where Professor Trombley lived. Someone had to warn him!

The boy left his flute and his music in the tower, raced down the ladder, hurdled the bells, and leaped down to a drift of snow on the roof. A blinding torrent of ice particles exploded in his face. Wiping his eyes, he made his way off the rooftop, jumped to the ground, and ran down the hill toward his friend's little house.

Tommy's sprained ankle pained him. His foot swelled in his boot as though it would split the leather, but still he ran. Sometimes the great drifts flung him back as he rushed toward them, and the tops swallowed him until only a patch of blue sky showed overhead, but he kept on. Half-swimming, half-rolling, he tried to climb over the top of any drift he could not wade through. "Please, oh, please! Somebody warn Professor Trombley!" he called out, but the wind generated by the fire now seized his cries, flinging them back in his face.

His sides ached, and his lungs burned. Tommy ran without even remembering to breathe. Drifts lay in his path like a series of giant waves frozen in some ocean storm. Up and down the street, a few people peered out from their houses to look about. When they saw that the fire threatened only the houses across the tracks, they retreated into the safety of their homes.

There were no footprints in front of Professor Trombley's little house. Flames licked up the shingles, and already smoke poured from a broken pane in the Professor's bedroom.

Tommy rushed up the steps and tried the door. Locked! He pounded hard, then began hurling himself against the door. First a crack appeared in the center, then the door appeared to give a little. With one great, desperate heave, Tommy split the door down the middle and tumbled into the smoky darkness within.

"Professor! Professor!" he screamed. "Are you in here?"

Face pressed close to the floor for air, Tommy crawled forward, groping for objects he might remember. There was a sudden explosion in the kitchen. A tongue of gas flame from the stove torched the far wall, illuminated the room for an instant, and went out.

"Professor!" In that brief flash of light, he had seen the old man lying face-down along the far wall. Rising to his knees and shielding his face from the heat, Tommy rushed to his friend, seized him by his collar, skidded him out the front door, and rolled him down the steps into a snowdrift. Not until the old man was safe did Tommy's own body begin to ache with the strain of his massive exertion.

Tommy pulled off his jacket and shielded Professor Trombley against the cold. For a moment, he thought the old man was dead, but then the Professor began to cough and choke.

"Professor! You're alive! Wake up! We've got to get

out of here before something else explodes!"

The old man's eyes fluttered for a moment before they opened wide. Orange light from the fire flickered in his face. "Tommy!" he exclaimed. "The fire! My music! I've got to get my music and my daughter's photograph! Help me up!"

The old man was almost to his feet when an explosion rocked the building and flung them both backward into the snow. Tommy jumped quickly to his friend's side, helped him up, and draped the old man's arm across his shoulders. "Let's get out of here, Maestro, before we fry!" He half-dragged, half-carried the old musician up a side street. Borrowing a toboggan from a front porch, he soon had the Professor stretched out on a couch in his mother's apartment.

"Thank goodness!" said Mrs. Parkman, pale with worry. "Thank goodness both of you are safe!" She put the kettle on the stove to boil and smiled gently at the Professor. "Welcome," she said. "Welcome to our home."

CHAPTER EIGHT

◆◆◆◆◆◆◆◆◆◆◆◆◆◆◆◆◆◆◆

The hallways were already deserted when Tommy plunged headlong down the slippery corridor, rushing to get to class before Mr. Eppridge, the history teacher, marked him tardy for the third time that month. Mercifully, he got his foot in the door just as it was swinging shut, slipped in, and plunked himself down in an empty seat.

First there was an astonished silence, then a titter of embarrassed giggles swelling to out-of-control laughter. Across the aisle from Tommy, a tall blonde girl turned to look at him, her face flaming with embarrassment. Betsy! What was she doing in his history class? Was she laughing at him, too? Where was Mr. Eppridge? Why weren't there any boys in this class? And where was his friend Corbyn, who usually saved him a seat?

"Welcome to Girl's Health and Hygiene." A woman

teacher addressed him as she turned from the blackboard. The trace of a smile worked the corners of her mouth. "You must be that new transfer student. What's your name again—Gladys something?"

The girls began to cheer while Tommy turned scarlet, wishing he could crawl under the desk. Seeing no escape through that sea of slender shoes, he jumped to his feet, upsetting the desk. He shot a mortified look at Betsy, nearly stripped the screws from the handle as he jerked the door open, and fled into the hall.

Moments later he was safely settled at his own desk in the room next door, and Mr. Eppridge was marking him tardy again.

"Rats, rats, and more rats!" He scolded himself as he slouched deep in his seat. Betsy must *really* be impressed with him now. He wondered how old he had to be to join the U.S. Cavalry in Montana. He pictured Betsy with tears in her eyes as she stared at a newspaper headline: "Local boy cited for extreme heroism in latest Indian uprising." Or, "Local boy chosen by Indians to replace famous chief!"

He longed for the rooftops, and he stared out the window at his private world until the brightness made his eyes water. The sound of baby pigeons being fed drifted in through an open window. When at last the bell put an end to his misery, he scurried down the hall for his next class, hoping none of the girls who had witnessed his awful mistake would recognize him.

For a few moments he became engulfed in a throng of students hurrying to their next classes and, not wanting to attract attention, missed the turn to the hall he wanted. Ahead of him, he could see Betsy caught up in a conversation with another girl, and he blushed hot to the roots of his hair. They were laughing, and he assumed they were laughing about him. He was relieved when he finally managed to extract himself from the crowd and get to his next class.

It was a class in music appreciation—one in which he could star. He realized suddenly that he was to play a duet with Elaine Rose this morning and he had forgotten his flute. Elaine was not as good as he, but she was plenty good nonetheless. He helped her all he could by passing on tips the Professor had taught him, and some days, when his concentration wavered, Elaine came close to edging him out for first chair.

He borrowed a flute from his friend Corbyn and sat down next to Elaine to play.

"Psssst!" Elaine whispered. "I hear you really wowed 'em in Girl's Hygiene. Wish I'd been there to see!"

As a hush fell over the class, Sir Tommy Parkman raised his flute dramatically—and botched his entrance so completely that Miss Grist, the teacher, ordered him to begin again.

"You wouldn't be nervous and upset about anything, would you, Tommy?" Elaine hissed. "Everybody, I mean *everybody*, says you have a crush on that awful Betsy Branch. Tommy! Oh, dear Tommy. Tell me it's not true! I'd die! I'd just *die* if it were!"

Tommy wiped the flute with a soft rag. Corbyn never cleaned his flute, and the keys often stuck. He pretended to examine one of them as if it had caused his failure.

Elaine reached over and flicked an imaginary speck of dust off first chair as though she would soon own it and wanted it to be clean. "I hear," she whispered as he raised his flute again, "I hear she's thinking of going steady with that dreadful Billy Patterson, the one who wins all the dance contests."

Tommy's music stand jerked spasmodically as he kicked its base and sent a shower of sheet music cascading across the classroom.

"Elaine," Miss Grist said severely, eyeing the mess, "our Mr. Parkman doesn't seem himself today. I suggest that you take over first chair."

"Sorry, old pal," Elaine gloated under her breath. "But talent will out, you know."

Elaine raised her flute and began to play, while Tommy played the second flute part along with her. It didn't matter one bit that Corbyn's father had gotten his flute in a pawn shop down on Lake Street. Faster and faster he played, until Elaine was working desperately to keep up. A trickle of sweat coursed down her forehead and stung one eye until she blinked. Her eyeglasses slid farther and farther down toward the end of her nose.

"Slow down!" Elaine hissed between solos, but a terrible gleam came to Tommy's eye, and his fingers flew even faster.

"I give up!" Elaine croaked, putting down her flute, her face flushed with anger. Suddenly, Tommy slowed and began to improvise, creating his own music out of his heart. The notes flowed sweet and slow and pure from some hidden well within him, sounds stored deeply in his shyness since childhood. In them were the solemn vespers of a hermit thrush on a summer's eve. The tremolo of a distant loon on a northern lake. And the two great sounds his father had loved the most—the call of a lonesome timber wolf cutting the thin, cold air of the Lake Superior country, and the loveliest, loneliest sound ever created by man—the whistle of a steam locomotive.

Miss Grist rose from her chair and stood swaying, holding the back of the chair for support. Her eyes were closed in concentration, and she seemed transported to some earlier, happier time. One by one, the members of Music Appreciation Two rose to their feet and stood in silent tribute, as though they realized suddenly that this bone-thin rag of a boy, whose fingers were often stained with soot, was a star rising in their midst.

CHAPTER NINE

◆◆◆◆◆◆◆◆◆◆◆◆◆◆◆◆◆◆◆◆

That week was a busy one for Tommy. The big blaze had stirred a fear of chimney fires in the minds of the townspeople. He could hardly keep up with the demand for service and still find time to do his homework. Biking from house to house after school, he would block any openings in the hearth with canvas to hold in the soot, then repair to the rooftops, set up his system of ropes and wire brushes, and proceed to scrape the buildup of soot and creosote into the fireplace, stove, or furnace below. Then he would shovel the residue into canvas bags and haul it away to the town dump.

There were a few people in town who knew enough to buy good wood and burn it hot, on occasion, to keep their chimneys fairly clean. But there were many who bought wet, green wood because it was cheap, and their chimneys became dangerously lined with creosote.

When a chimney fire started, it often burned so hot that it weakened the mortar between the bricks, and the house sometimes burned down before help could arrive. The thunder of a chimney fire at its peak was awesome.

Tommy felt sorry for Professor Trombley. The Maestro had lost everything he owned in the fire, and he had no relatives.

"You're going to stay on with us," Tommy told him.

The old man protested, but to no avail. Tommy took the living room couch and gave Professor Trombley his bedroom.

"I like this!" Tommy explained, to make the old man feel at home. "I've got a live-in music teacher!"

Things did indeed seem brighter. "Maybe I do have to work a little harder at my music," the boy explained to his mother one night, "but I'm learning fast. When I've got a question, the Professor is always right there with an answer. With his help, my flute's going much better, and he's teaching me a lot about composing. He's easy enough to have around, too, even if he does get a little drifty sometimes."

"Chautauqua!" the old man said one night. "Tommy, what wouldn't I give to have you spend a summer there? My friend Boris conducts the symphony. You could play the flute and help conduct. You'd get real experience as a composer. I had a little leather sack of Spanish doubloons. Pure gold, you know. I would use them to send you to Chautauqua, but I think they burned up in the fire. You know about the fire I had?"

"Yes, Professor," Tommy said patiently. "I know

about the fire." He also knew about the Professor's coins. The old man had given them away two summers ago to help a family get medical attention for their daughter.

"I must tell Miss Jenny Lind about you," the Professor went on. "They call her 'the Swedish Nightingale,' you know. The next time I go to see her, I'll take you along and get you an audition. What a glorious voice she has! Spectacular! And when she hears you play, lad, she'll jump at the chance to help."

"I'd like to meet her," Tommy said, knowing full well that Jenny Lind's great voice had been silenced by death some years before.

That night Tommy skipped practicing with the Professor and climbed to his little room in the church tower. Music ran rampant through his brain, leaving him tense and frustrated when he could not get it written down. He was already on the third movement of his symphony. This movement captured the anger—the hatred of one person for another, one family for another, one church for another. He portrayed the jealousy, the avarice, and the passions—sometimes violent and dangerous.

At ten o'clock, the Episcopal bells started ringing and immediately began to quarrel with those of the Catholics. So great was the disharmony that Tommy felt sick to his stomach and could hardly wait for the last peal. "I know what's wrong!" he thought. "All the discord I hear in the bells makes for unhappiness in this town. Maybe it's up to me to find a cure!"

He left his little study, slid to a low roof, then dropped

to a courtyard. His ankle still pained him, but these last few days he had pretty much come to accept the pain as a part of his life.

A light still showed in the furnace room where Mr. Carlisle, the church maintenance man, sat dreaming on a pile of newspapers. The door was open a crack, and Tommy watched as orange light from the fire in the furnace played across the man's face.

Asleep! Tommy peered in again. The man's toolbox lay open by his chair. Tommy crept in and borrowed a set of files from the box, then tiptoed out. The door squealed a protest as he tried to shut it quietly behind him. Mr. Carlisle muttered in his sleep, stirred himself into a more comfortable position, and relaxed.

Once he had climbed again to the bell tower, Tommy took out his pocketknife and tapped each of the four bells, memorizing the tones. With a clean new file, he began reshaping the lip of one of the bells, catching the brass filings in a rusty garbage can lid he found in a corner of the belfry. So concentrated was the boy that a waking pigeon, flushing from a ledge above him, startled him into dropping the first file down through a crack in the floor.

Every now and then, as he filed on, Tommy paused to tap the bell with the back of his pocketknife. At first there was no perceptible change in tone, but gradually, as the pile of brass filings grew, this bell sounded more in harmony with the bell he had selected as the norm.

A brisk north wind off the lake chilled him to the bone, and the cold steel of the file drained what little warmth Tommy could keep in his gloved fingers. Time and again, he had to waste precious minutes by climbing to his hideaway in the tower and thawing out his limbs. But he always went back to his job, and soon the whole lip of the bell gleamed brightly with his efforts.

When at last the two bells harmonized perfectly, Tommy began on the third. He frowned as he tapped it. This bell was wildly out of tune with the others, and he hoped he could change the pitch enough to make a difference. Snow had started to fall again. Big wet flakes sailed into the belfry, melted on his cap, and drenched the shoulders of his jacket.

Far below, he heard the stable doors slide open down at the city yard. He listened attentively to the voices of teamsters and heard the scrape of steel on cobblestones as the drivers adjusted their blades for the night's road plowing. The hammering of shod horses' hooves on rock was muffled in part by the thickly falling snow.

Switching the clappers between the last two remaining bells seemed to help. Tommy filed and filed, until a great pile of gleaming brass dust lay upon his rusted tray. But the pitch was still not true. He started higher on the side of the bell, attacking the black, weathered surface with all his strength as he sought the bare metal underneath. He looked at his pocket watch. Just an hour and ten minutes to go before the bells sounded for morning service, and he was a long way from finished. There was no time to creep up to the tower room and get warm.

He heard the rumble of wagon wheels and the squeak of a dry hub. Jim Briley was up early, driving a buckboard over to his livery stable on the main street, where he'd feed his horses and open for business. Jim did a land-office business as a wheelwright, fixing wheels for travelers, but he often neglected to grease the hubs on his own wagon.

After a little tinkering here and there with the file, three bells were done. Tommy started on the fourth with a vengeance. The bell was less sheltered than the others and more corroded. Here and there, impurities in the metal itself had combined with drifting pollution from the local smelter, covering patches of the bell with a green patina. Thirty minutes to go, then twenty-five.

Tommy ignored the fierceness of the storm and the lashing sleet that forced him to work with his eyes half-closed. He took out his knife again and tapped the bell. He frowned. Still more filing to do.

Three minutes short of eight! He looked about, surprised that daylight had crept upon him. He filed hard for a moment, checked the pitch, filed again, then smiled his satisfaction when the sound pleased his critical ear.

Dashing for the warmth of his tiny study, Tommy had barely taken off his wet gloves and seated himself in front of the little stove when the great bells began to sound their morning call to worship. *Bong! Bong! Bong! Bong!* went the four bells, each one harmonizing perfectly with the others.

CHAPTER TEN

◆◆◆◆◆◆◆◆◆◆◆◆◆◆◆◆◆◆◆◆◆

Tommy wanted to hear the Episcopal bells finish their ringing, but it was not to happen. Just after those great bells began to toll, the Catholic bells sounded their discord down the street, joined by the Presbyterian and the Methodists—all competing in another great argument. As he listened in despair, Tommy knew he had his work cut out for him. He would not rest until all the bells were filed and ringing in perfect harmony.

The Catholic bells would be tough. They seemed all but inaccessible in their tower. The only access was by climbing an iron stairway that was guarded by a locked door of heavy steel. And that roof! Its pitch was so steep that, if you got tired climbing, you could lean against it to rest. And ice! For all the heat the church put on its congregation, not much escaped to warm the roof above.

That morning, the boy walked around the Catholic church and looked at it from all angles. He saw a priest coming down the sidewalk and almost panicked, as though his plans were written all over his face. But the priest merely nodded to him and said gently, "It's a fine building, is it not?"

"It *will* be," Tommy thought, "when I've had a chance to fix those doggone bells."

On the north side of the church, Tommy's heart leaped. Some workmen were repairing the slate roof, cleaning gutters and scraping moss. The project might take them another week, and though they might take down their ladder at night, surely they would leave their elaborate scaffolding in place.

Tommy stood looking up into a frozen elm tree as though looking at birds, but in reality he was planning his ascent of the tower.

"What bird be you looking at, son?" It was the priest again, returned from his walk.

"Why, it's a red-eyed vireo, Father."

"A *what?* Red-eyed! Faith, you don't suppose he's been tippling, do you, down at the local saloon?"

The priest went off, chuckling at his joke, unaware that it was too cold for vireos and scarcely dreaming of what the soot-smudged boy had in mind.

That night, Tommy returned under the cover of darkness with a bundle of strong ropes in hand and the set of files secure in his belt. The workmen had taken down their ladder and propped it along the base of the church. The boy had a hard time putting it back up by himself. He hoped there was no one in the church who might hear the scraping of the steel hooks against the stone wall as he forced the ladder into place.

Quickly, Tommy climbed the rungs, gained the scaffolding, and scampered to the roof. The black ice was crisp under his feet as he threw a rope around a vent pipe, pulled himself to the ridgecap, and straddled it as if he were riding a horse.

Tommy suddenly lay low against the icy roof. A police wagon, pulled by a team of iron-gray Percherons, came driving up the alley, its driver beaming first one building then another with his lantern. "Oh, no!" Tommy whispered under his breath. The big reflectors focused the light on the ladder, casting strange shadows on the wall of the church.

"Whoa!" a gruff voice commanded the horses. Two constables with torches got off the wagon and approached. Completely exposed, Tommy clung to the roof, hoping they wouldn't look up.

The men took down the ladder and laid it alongside the building, then went back to their wagon. Only when they had driven off down the alley and the sound of hoofbeats had faded did the boy dare move.

Time and again, Tommy threw a rope with a grappling hook at the sill of the bell tower. Each time, the hook failed to catch and fell back toward him. His arm began to ache with the strain. He backed up along the roof and widened the angle of his throw. This time, the hook sailed into the bell tower and struck one of the bells with a fearful clang. Mercifully, it bounced back, hooked the sill, and held. The boy tested the rope and found it solid. Not daring to look down, he went up the rope and over the lip like a squirrel on a bird feeder.

Quickly, he tapped each instrument with his pocketknife and memorized its pitch. There were six huge bells, but two of them were right on pitch. On one, the rope had been purposely tied back to keep the bell from ringing. When Tommy tested it, he found out why. It was so miserably out of tune that the bell ringer had abandoned all hope of using it.

Tommy started on that bell first. Soon the scale fell away, and the rim of the bell began to look clean and bright. It was peaceful in the tower, and he was so far above the ground that no one would hear his filing and scraping.

A cold wind off Lake Superior occasionally ruffled the feathers of the sleeping pigeons overhead, and now and again one would awaken and start cooing. Tommy worked steadily, pausing now and then to warm his fingers and beat his hands against his thighs to ease the cramps. The second and third bells were fairly easy, but the fourth seemed of a harder cast, resisting his efforts to hurry and be gone.

Eventually, the big casting fell to his assault and came in tune with the rest. The boy tapped each bell once more to be sure, then tied a fresh knot in the arm of the abandoned bell. He smiled to himself, picturing how astonished the bell ringer would be if that long-silent bell joined the others in song.

Even though the ladder now lay on the ground, Tommy made short work of his descent, dropping down the roof on doubled ropes, which made it easy to pull them down after him as soon as he had descended that particular segment. Even the jump from the roof to the ground was little trouble, thanks to a particularly tall snowdrift piled against one wall.

The boy was back in his bed when the bells sounded in the distance for early mass. He turned his head on the pillow to listen, and smiled with satisfaction as these bells, too, pealed in perfect harmony.

CHAPTER ELEVEN

◆◆◆◆◆◆◆◆◆◆◆◆◆◆◆◆◆◆◆◆

It was a fine though unstable morning in late April when Tommy climbed to his secret room above the bell tower and began the last movement of his symphony. He felt as important as a setter pup pointing to its first butterfly.

Now that three movements were behind him, Tommy wrote with a confidence he had never known before. The music felt good to him, and he suspected it *was* good, although only a real performance by an orchestra would tell.

From his hideaway, he could hear the fracturing of the ice fields on Lake Superior and a distant groaning, as sheet piled on sheet ahead of the wind. He heard the booming surf as the big lake freed itself from its winter shackles and started to make waves once again. Out on the breakwater, the foghorn was chasing away the last vestiges of a night mist; steam locomotives were chugging along the docks; iron ore was rumbling down chutes into the holds of ore boats. Even the distant melancholy *whoot* of an incoming freighter fighting the drift ice seemed a harbinger of better weather ahead.

The streets were filled with horses. Hackneys pulled carriages. Big draft horses, necks bowed, leaned into their loads but still managed a friendly whinny to a passing stablemate. Prancing saddle mounts were glad to be out of their winter stalls.

The sparrows, which had wintered on grain that fell from the nosebags of Mr. Stinglein's delivery horses, now fought over crumbs from children's lunches. Pigeons flew about gables and cornices, looking for winter-broken windows that would lend access to attics in which they could nest. Never satisfied with the weather, a pair of robins sat high in the leafing elms and petitioned the heavens for rain.

There had been a slight delay in Tommy's effort to tune the last of the church bells when Pastor Lindquist caught him climbing the roof of the Lutheran church and ordered him down. There was somewhat more of a to-do when Tommy attempted to explain his set of files by telling the pastor he had to carry them because his fingernails grew so fast.

Tommy might have ended up before a magistrate had he not remembered cleaning the pastor's chimney and overhearing certain comments the minister made to his wife about the stinginess of one of the leading vestrymen on the church board. The pastor was conveniently away tending the sick when the boy scrambled back up the roof, and soon the little bells were ringing in harmony.

Now Tommy sat in his secret room, pouring his heart into his music. He opened the vents and let the spring breezes sweep out the stale breath of winter. The voice of the season's first song sparrow, a bit rusty from disuse, floated up to him on air currents redolent with the familiar odor of lawns just freed from the gloom of sooty snowbanks.

Such a fluttering of tiny notes on the page! Tommy wondered how they could ever convey the sound and the fury he was imagining. Could he possibly translate smells, sounds, thoughts, and emotions onto paper, so that some far-off musician who had never known northern Michigan might turn the notes into music, music into mood, and mood into imagery that every listener would understand despite their vastly different experiences?

"That, my boy, is a mark of genius," the Professor said when Tommy related his doubts and fears. "Think of what Tchaikovsky did in the *Pathetique*, merely through the use of minor chords. We feel the pain! Aye, that's the test!"

Sometimes Tommy was dragged down by his flickering doubts, but when he picked up his flute and played back the most impassioned sections, his fears would vanish. He would surge ahead at such times, composing with a surety and confidence far beyond his years. He often felt as though some great composer, long dead, was writing music through him, thus gaining one last chance to give the world a rare gift.

The bells, however, eluded him. How could he reduce the great, rolling peals of iron and bronze to mere flyspecks on a page? How could trombones, trumpets, clarinets, violas, violins, cymbals, drums, and the other instruments possibly recreate the beauty of the original sounds?

And now he wondered how he could convey the changes he was suddenly seeing all over town. Could they be real? All winter long the Smiths had been bickering over nothing. Tommy had hated to clean their chimney because of the senseless arguments that drifted up their flue. But that very morning, Tommy had seen them walking hand in hand down Elm Street, not caring who saw them, past middle age and back in love.

Out there on the big road, he had watched a freighter actually stop his horses to help a buggy owner change a wheel in a mudhole.

And was the rumor true? That Mrs. Casper had been seen carrying a tray of hot food to old Mrs. Haskall's house, humming a melody as she skipped along?

Tommy climbed down through the trap door and leaned on the bells, taking a new look at the town. Over in the park children were actually playing and laughing! And Kitty Lennin, who hadn't been out of her wheelchair all winter, was crawling on her hands and knees in her garden, setting out petunias. Two streets over, he recognized Mr. Posenke, playing catch with his son. Mr. Posenke had not spoken three words to his son in four years!

The bells! It had to be true that the bells, now playing

in harmony, were changing the town. Overwhelmed by excitement, Tommy scrambled up the ladder, seized his pen, and grabbed one last handful of paper. Ten hours later, as the sun cast its last rosy rays above the tree-tops, he finished his symphony. He quickly bundled the sheaves of paper into his arms and headed off to find the Professor. The hour of reckoning had arrived. Now his work must stand on its own and be judged.

CHAPTER TWELVE

◆◆◆◆◆◆◆◆◆◆◆◆◆◆◆◆◆◆◆◆◆

The news that John Branch had gotten his hands on the last of the lots along the lakeshore came as no surprise to the townspeople. Rumor had it that the lovely little cove along Lake Superior, where a generation of folks had been wont to picnic, would be dredged and deepened for an iron ore dock. The tall groves of white pines that had protected the town from savage north winds off the lake would be cut for dock pilings.

Professor Trombley sighed deeply as he signed a contract with Branch's lawyer for purchase of his lot and the charred ruin of what had been his daughter's house.

"I'll miss the place," the Maestro confessed later to Tommy. "It seems that only yesterday we walked those lovely woods, my daughter and I. We stood together on that little bridge across the stream, listened to birds singing in the woods, and watched the shadows of trout swimming upstream to spawn. Well, I'm not young enough or rich enough to stand in the way of progress."

They were walking together on a hill above the town, Tommy and the Professor, when the old musician turned to the boy and smiled. "I guess you're wondering what I thought of your symphony," he said. "I've gone over it, you know. Note by note."

Tommy faced him suddenly. "It's bad, isn't it? I know it's bad, but I'll write another one. I know I can do better."

For a long moment Professor Trombley looked at him and said nothing. Then he smiled. "It's good," he said. "You let me see the wind! In the first movements, I wondered at the pain, understood for the first time how life had wounded you, how your father hurt you by what he did. By the third movement, you had overcome your fears and shyness. You were bold, blaming no one for what life had dealt you. You were determined to lift the world about you, whether it wanted to be lifted or not. And the last movement? Serenity, my boy. Life as it could be, if only we would reach!

"It needs work, of course," the Professor went on. "But I could help with that. Your woodwinds are a delight, and the French horns are magnificent, but your violins are a mite weak. You must give them a chance to speak for you!"

The Professor seated himself on a great, mossy log, all that remained of a giant white pine that had once dominated this headland overlooking the lake. "I have your manuscript here," he said, patting his briefcase. "I wanted to keep it longer, but I know it is your only copy. I feared that something might happen to it, and all your hard work would be for nothing."

As the old man unstrapped his tattered briefcase, a look of fear flooded his eyes. Before he had even finished opening the case, both of them knew the awful truth. The manuscript was gone!

CHAPTER THIRTEEN

◆◆◆◆◆◆◆◆◆◆◆◆◆◆◆◆◆◆◆◆◆

As they hurried to retrace the Professor's steps, Tommy put his hand on the old man's shoulders. "It's all right," he said. "We'll find the manuscript. If we don't, why, I'll just sit down and write another one, even better than the first." Tommy's voice trembled at the thought, and the Professor seemed to feel even worse than before.

"I had it this morning, and the only place I opened my briefcase was at Branch's office when I turned over the deed to my property. I don't know how on earth it could have fallen out without my noticing."

Tears welled in Tommy's eyes, but he turned his head quickly so the old man wouldn't notice. He'd worked so hard that his brain was still numb from exhaustion. At this point, he wasn't sure he had another symphony left in him.

John Branch's office took up the whole first floor of a huge brick building. Grim concrete gargoyles stared down at them as they moved up the front steps. Tommy felt shabby and out of place in such splendor. He glanced down at his hands and was relieved to see that they were clean. Elegant paintings of hunting scenes hung from the walls, while bronze statues of galloping horses stood atop slender columns of marble.

"May I help you?" A tall lady rose behind a big cherrywood desk and stepped quickly toward them. Her dress was as black as the inside of a chimney, and her long skirts went *swish, swish, swish* as she walked. Her eyes, like those of a hunting eagle, missed no detail.

"May I help you?" she said again, but her tone seemed to ask, "What are you doing here?"

"I was wondering...," Professor Trombley stammered. "That is to say...I was here earlier this morning. Mr. Dore of Acquisitions met with me. I sold Mr. Branch some property, and I may have inadvertently left a manuscript here belonging to my young friend. Please, could I see Mr. Dore? It's terribly urgent!"

"Mr. Dore will be gone until next week. I suggest you come back then." She moved toward a small table of polished marble and began writing. "I'll put a note in Mr. Dore's box. I'm sure, however, that if you had left such a manuscript, Mr. Dore would have given it to me."

"Think, Professor! You've got to think hard," Tommy said when they were back on the street. "Did you stop for tea anywhere? At the inn, perhaps? Did you sit down to rest on a bench in the park? Could the music have fallen out as you walked along? You're...well, kind of absentminded, you know."

"No!" the Professor said firmly, answering all of Tommy's questions at once.

The boy clutched his flute case to his chest, as though absorbing courage. "I guess I'll have to go talk to Mr. Branch himself," he said finally.

Professor Trombley stared at him. "He wouldn't talk to you. You'll never get past that dreadful woman!"

"You'll see," the boy replied, bounding up the steps as though every leap strengthened his resolve.

This time the woman hardly looked up from her papers.

"I want to talk to Mr. Branch himself!" Tommy blurted.

"He's not in," she said flatly. "He's in Europe. Go peddle your papers somewhere else."

"He's in," Tommy retorted. "I can smell his cigar. That is, unless it's yours."

He took his flute out of its case.

"What are you doing?" the woman exclaimed, leaping from her seat and scattering papers across the floor. "Mr. Branch hates music!"

"What does that matter," Tommy said, raising his flute, "if he's over in Europe?"

The boy smiled and began a favorite passage from his own symphony. He was back on Branch's rooftop, playing his heart out to Betsy somewhere in that big house below.

"Don't!" the woman said weakly, slumping back into her seat. "Put that thing down!"

The big door behind the desk swung open. There

stood Mr. Branch and Betsy.

"Mr. Branch!" Tommy said, putting down his flute. "I've got to talk to you, sir." He half-raised his flute again as though threatening to play if he were refused an audience.

"This morning, sir, Professor Trombley came to your office to sign some papers. In his briefcase, he had the only copy of a symphony I've composed. Now he's lost it, and I've got to have it back! Please, sir. It's got to be around here someplace!"

Boom! Boom! Boom! went the Episcopal bells. *Bong! Bong! Bong!* went the Catholic bells. Mr. Branch's hands flew up to his ears, as though from force of habit. Then his expression changed. He seemed puzzled that the bells were not giving him his usual headache, but fearful that it might start at any moment.

"It was my first symphony," Tommy said when the bells had ceased.

Betsy, who had been shuffling some papers over by the desk, looked over and gave him a shy smile.

"Professor Trombley was helping me with it. He had it in his briefcase this morning when he did some business with Mr. Dore, who works for you. The Professor's getting old and kind of forgetful, but he swears he left the manuscript here."

Mr. Branch stood silently, regarding the boy as though inspecting his clothes. Tommy wondered, suddenly, if he had a smear of soot on the end of his nose.

There was another pause while the Lutheran bells tinkled their silvery little tune. It was light and airy, and the melody seemed to fill the whole office with sunshine. There was one bell, Tommy noticed, that was the tiniest, teeniest bit off. A pass or two with a file would fix it when he got around to it.

"What's your name, young man?" Mr. Branch's eyes bore down on the young musician.

"Tommy Parkman, sir."

"This is my daughter, Betsy. She'll help you find those papers. *If* they're here!"

The man swept back into his office and closed the door behind him with a resounding slam.

Tommy had never walked beside Betsy before, and she seemed smaller than he had thought. He tripped over a rug and caught himself just in time.

"I suppose we ought to look on Mr. Dore's desk," Betsy said. "Maybe your music's there." She turned to look at him. "I hope you find it. I've heard you sometimes, playing on the roofs where no one can see. So beautiful! It's like birds singing up there."

"I like being up high," Tommy said. "You can see way out on Lake Superior. I can see the ore boats out there way before anybody else knows they're coming. All the sounds of the town float up there like music, and all I have to do is write them down. That's what my symphony is about—the town."

"We'll find it!" Betsy said. "I know we will."

But Mr. Dore's desk was bare of all but some steel-nibbed pens and an ink pot. His wastebasket had been emptied. One by one, Betsy opened drawers and looked through files. Nothing even vaguely resembled Tommy's manuscript.

"Don't you have some original notes?" Betsy asked.

"I could copy them for you." Her face flushed with shyness. "I've been trying to write songs—not a great big symphony like yours, but songs. I wanted to study under the Professor, but he said he didn't have time for me right now. But I could help you rewrite your symphony."

Tommy shook his head sadly. "I burned them," he said. "I didn't dream that I might lose the manuscript. Every scrap of paper with a musical note on it is gone—burned up in a little stove I have."

Betsy was about to lead him out of Mr. Dore's office when she suddenly stopped and squealed. "Look, Tommy! Look under the desk!"

There, all in a pile on the floor, lay Tommy's manuscript.

Chapter Fourteen

◆◆◆◆◆◆◆◆◆◆◆◆◆◆◆◆◆

"It should go *this* way!" the Professor said. "*Pum, pum, pumtady, pum, pum, PUM!* Lots more brass here. Let the violins rest a moment."

Tommy sagged back in his chair. For twelve straight hours, he had been working with the Professor on the symphony. His brain felt like a piece of stale suet in a bird feeder. "No," he said weakly. "That's not what my music was trying to show. There's an argument coming up the chimney here. The brass is fine for Old Man Schaeffer. He's trying to bully Mrs. Schaeffer into letting him have a night off with the boys, but she's violins, and she's doing a good job of fighting back. I can't let her just sit there and take it."

"Mmm," said Professor Trombley, which meant he was not quite convinced but was willing to put the matter off. He pulled his watch from his vest and inspected it for a moment. "An hour left of daylight," he said. "A short walk in the countryside will help me sleep. Let's put the music away until tomorrow, Tommy, and enjoy the beauties of nature."

"Fiddle!" Tommy said. "I know you! There's that pretty little meadow down near where your house once stood, and you can't stay away from it. But Old Man Branch is changing things down there. For weeks now, I've seen freight wagons headed down Alder Road with loads of lumber. Buggy traffic, too. Someone told me one of those fancy architects is in town that Branch brought up clear from Chicago. You'd best stay away from that meadow if you don't want a broken heart!"

But the Professor prevailed, and they went for their walk. Far off in the distance, they heard the slow, measured boom of surf crashing on the harbor breakwater. "Listen!" the old man said. "Right out of your symphony. You caught it all so beautifully, my boy."

A brown thrasher poured its heart out from some hidden tangle in the shrubbery, and Tommy thrilled to its music. There was such beauty here on this headland overlooking the lake, its wild meadows ringed with ancient pines. He hated John Branch for buying the Professor's property. This is where the old musician should have spent the rest of his days.

A morning cloak butterfly wandered erratically over the evening grassland as though looking for its perch from the previous night. Deep in thought, Tommy's eyes followed the fluttering creature almost without seeing. That John Branch! Next time he saw that man, he'd give him a piece of his mind, even if he *was* Betsy's father.

Thlot, thlot. They heard the sound of steel horseshoes striking rock. Suddenly, a buggy came around the bend, drawn by a handsome bay. Betsy held the reins, and beside her sat her father, giving her driving lessons.

"Slow down, girl!" John Branch commanded. But Betsy, with the breeze blowing through her long, blonde hair, seemed determined to keep the horse at a trot.

"I'm going to tell him!" Tommy said angrily to the Professor. "I'll tell that old bag of bones he had no right to take this meadow away from you. You spent your lifetime bringing music to people and helping folks out. What has he ever done for anyone?"

The Professor looked about for a place to hide. "Don't you dare, Tommy! You're not to say a word to him, you understand? Oh, my goodness! Here they come right toward us. Please! Lift your hat as they pass, but don't open your mouth. There are things you just don't understand!"

But Tommy leaped up on a stump and stood almost at eye level with Betsy and her father. He held up his hand, signaling them to stop, and Betsy pulled in the horse with a nervous little "Whoa."

"Don't make waves!" Tommy heard his mother's voice come from somewhere within, pleading with him, ever fearful of losing their home. But Tommy was determined to be heard.

"Please, sir," the Professor apologized before Tommy could speak. "He's just a boy! He doesn't know what you have in mind. I was going to tell him, but I wanted it to be a surprise."

"Mr. Branch!" Tommy stood straight and tall on his stump, looking at Betsy's father. "I have something I want to tell you. Please do me the courtesy, sir, of listening.

"There was a time," Tommy told the unsmiling banker, "when the crowned heads of Europe stood clapping to honor Professor Trombley and the music he produced. He conducted the finest orchestras and brought joy to the hearts of thousands of people. For the Professor, the likes of Jenny Lind gave the finest performances of their lives!"

Tommy glanced down at the stump as though fearful of falling off, then looked at Betsy, who was staring at him, open-mouthed, tugging at her tresses. Her father, meanwhile, sat with arms folded on his buggy throne, looking a bit like an emperor.

"Oh, my heavens!" the Professor moaned, plunking himself down on a convenient roadside log. His face was awash in mortification. "Everything is lost. Everything!"

"The Professor chose to honor this town," Tommy went on, "by retiring here. All he wanted in return for a lifetime of giving was a chance to live here in his humble little cottage. But fire burned down his house, sir, and now he lives with my mother and me in our little apartment above a church. The final blow, Mr. Branch, was when you bought all this land. To make more money, sir, when you already had plenty!"

"Oh, murder! Murder! It's all over!" the Professor moaned, sagging deeper into his seat on the log.

Tommy was startled to see John Branch smile. "Get down off your stump, young scoundrel," he commanded.

"You and Professor Trombley—jump up here on the wagon. There's plenty of room for everyone. Betsy! Turn the carriage around. You can do it." He smiled down at the old man as he offered him a hand. "Professor, I think it's time we showed this young man our dream."

Our dream? What was this? Was the Professor involved with John Branch in some odious real estate scheme? Tommy glanced at Betsy, but all he could see was the back of her pretty head as she let the horse step into a trot down the road.

"Whoa!" Betsy said as they swept around a bend. There, on the far edge of the Professor's favorite meadow, stood a perfect replica of the little house that had burned down. And beyond the cottage, overlooking the great cove on Lake Superior, workmen were beginning to build what appeared to be a great outdoor stage.

"The John Trombley Music Center!" Betsy's father announced proudly. "Biggest concert stage in the whole Midwest. You see those granite cliffs there, young Tommy? That's what makes the place work. Perfect acoustics! Perfect! I've had experts in from Europe. The Professor set up the contacts for me."

Betsy glanced back shyly at Tommy as her father went on. "Never would have found this place if it hadn't been for those blasted bells. I used to leave town just before they rang. Gave me headaches. Perfect pitch can be a curse, as you may know. One day I was down here looking the place over for factory sites, and the bells caught me off guard. I tried covering my ears, but it was no use. Then I suddenly realized that my ears didn't hurt anymore. The music was beautiful." He took his spectacles off his nose, squinted at them, blew off a speck of road dust, and replaced them.

"Betsy here got in touch with the Professor, and he told me about you. I had the constable investigate, and it was just as we suspected. There were file marks on the bells. Someone had gone to a lot of trouble. To my mind, young man, the town owes you a great deal!"

But Tommy was not really listening. From a grove of hemlocks along the lakeshore, a hermit thrush was pouring out its soul. Tommy took his flute from its case and held it for a moment. He'd play it in a minor key, of course. How else could he express the thrush's exquisite outpourings? Or the feeling of northern solitude? The notes came spilling wildly out of nowhere into his head. Smiling at Betsy, he raised the flute to his lips and began to play.

CHAPTER FIFTEEN

◆◆◆◆◆◆◆◆◆◆◆◆◆◆◆◆◆◆◆◆◆◆

A half hour before concert time, Tommy sat in the men's dressing room beneath the grand wooden stage and worked at tying his bow tie.

"Ridiculous!" snorted the Professor. "Here you are, a great composer, and you look like a tramp." He grabbed the loose end of the black bow tie and pulled it off the boy's neck. "Start over. And when you have the tie right, let me brush the dog hair off your tuxedo, or I may have to lead you onto the stage with a leash. You've been wrestling with Betsy's collie again. And your nails! Of all days to go off on the rooftops, cleaning chimneys!"

Tommy grinned. The Professor was even more nervous than he was, and was trying to mask his condition by pretending to be stern.

He finished dressing, submitted to the Professor's

brushing, and peered out the window. Already he could see long lines of carriages, and folks spreading blankets on the vast lawns beneath the park lights. This was going to be different from playing in the little German band down at the city park!

His mother had made some new friends at the church, and he could see them now, setting up a picnic just a cabbage throw away from the stage.

It had taken four long months to get ready. Four months of working with the Professor, cutting and rewriting the symphony until the notes on the page blurred before his eyes and he wished he had never undertaken such a task. Sometimes he even suspected that the old man was trying to *destroy* the music instead of fine-tuning it. But in the end, Tommy always had to admit that it was better.

"Even a thrush has to learn how to sing," Professor Trombley told him.

The crowd out there was in a festive mood. Fragments of conversations drifted in through the open windows. Children laughed and played, wives traded recipes, and husbands blew the foam off steins of beer. Soon all the hitching racks were filled, and attendants directed carriages and riders into an empty field across the road.

"I can't believe this is happening!" Tommy thought, hugging his flute to his chest. "Some of these folks are even from out of town!"

Professor Trombley was calling the orchestra members together. "My friends!" he told the musicians as they gathered. "My friends, this is the very first performance of the very first symphony written by our young friend here. You will remember it as the start of a great musical career. Play well! Give him an evening he'll never forget!"

As Tommy ascended the stage and took his place next to Elaine Rose in the flute section, his stiff collar seemed so tight that he wondered how he would get enough air to play.

"Pssst!" said Elaine. "Here comes that Betsy Branch you're so stuck on. What's she doing coming up on the stage? She's no musician. Why, she couldn't carry a tune in a coal scuttle!"

Tommy tried not to stare. Betsy wore a long black dress and seated herself along one wall, where workmen had installed a big wooden box.

"What on earth is that contraption?" Tommy asked.

"It's a telephone," Elaine sniffed. "So she can call her boyfriends and laugh at you when the audience starts pelting you with ripe tomatoes."

Tommy ignored Elaine. The box fascinated him. He could see a single wire stretching up to a series of tall poles that seemed to lead back to town. Another wire ran from the box to an iron pipe driven into the earth just beside the stage. A telephone! It was rumored that John Branch had invested heavily in the Bell Telephone Company. He claimed that someday there would be a telephone in every house in town!

Betsy and the Professor had been thick as thieves lately, but why that machine? Why was Betsy onstage, anyway, and whom was she going to call? She'd never even come to a rehearsal, yet here she was.

As if to confuse him more, Betsy looked over her

shoulder and smiled at him. His face grew hot, and his hands were so clammy that the flute almost slipped from his fingers.

"Did you see that smile? Did you see that smile she gave the trombone player?" Elaine giggled. "Eat your heart out, Tommy. She's probably in love with him!"

"That smile was for me," Tommy thought, but he kept silent and let a few moments elapse before he glanced over his shoulder to see if Betsy might have been smiling at someone else. He was relieved to see that the trombone section was far to the left.

Elaine kept buzzing in his ear about Betsy, but he tuned her out as though she were only a persistent gnat. He wished suddenly that he were somewhere else—like up on the rooftops above the waterworks, listening to the night waves lapping against the breakwater. Here, all eyes were upon him—the chimney sweep who had dared write a symphony.

With his eyes, he traced an escape route. Past the bassoons and the French horns, over the side of the stage, down past the line of carriages, up that big red oak tree to that low shed, across that roof to Finnegan's Storage, then by rope to the Froebel School.

But then there was no time to flee. He heard the crowd grow suddenly still, and he saw the snowy head of the Professor as he climbed the stairs to command the stage.

CHAPTER SIXTEEN

♦♦♦♦♦♦♦♦♦♦♦♦♦♦♦♦♦♦♦♦

The old Maestro bounded up the steps to the podium with surprising grace. The audience applauded politely, as though not quite convinced they were about to hear something special. Tommy heard his name mentioned, but he shut it out, not really knowing whether to look down at the floor modestly or stare out over the audience. He wished the Professor would stop talking and get on with it.

The gas lamps flickered and dimmed, while the audience fell silent once again as Professor Trombley raised his baton.

Clip clop, clippity-clop! Clip clop, clippity-clop went the coconut shells, giving Tommy's musical rendition of Mr. Stinglein's old horse pulling the milk wagon up Arch Street. *Clip, clop, clippity-clop! Clippity, clippity, clop, clop, clop!*

"Hey! Danged if that don't sound like Old Stinglein's delivery horse!" said Jesse Mudge, relieved to find something familiar in the program. "Why, I'd know that sound anywhere!"

"Shhh!" went the crowd around him, fixing him with glares.

Next came the violins, strings dusty with rosin, imitating a flock of purple grackles disturbed in their early morning slumber by dawn, which was represented by a whole bank of French horns.

"Why, I wake up every morning of my summer to just that sound!" cried old Ezzard Banks. "You hear that flock of grackles, Bud?" he hollered to a friend about twenty feet away. "Say, I reckon all those folks who told me this was going to be a wasted evening was plumb wrong. Now *that's* what I call music!"

"Shhhhhh!" went the crowd about him.

"Sea gulls! Them's my favorites. Listen to them gulls, would you? Bet they're headed to the city dump right this minute!" Jake Malloy spilled hot coffee on his britches as the bassoons became a flock of gulls.

"Shhhhhhhhh!" went the crowd, trying to concentrate.

At Professor Trombley's signal, Tommy rose to his feet, adjusted his music stand, and raised his magic flute.

"Show 'em what you can do!" Elaine whispered up at him, finally on Tommy's side.

Tommy managed a glance at Betsy. She was smiling at *him* now. There wasn't anyone in back of him. When he launched into his flute solo, he was playing just for her, and no one else existed in the whole world.

His music was the spring wind blowing sweet and pure off Lake Superior. It was wind tasting of loneliness, wind fresh from the Arctic that had never known the bitterness of coal smoke and had never rattled dry autumn leaves in a backyard.

The faces in the audience went soft and tender. Hands reached out and held, wife to husband, child to parent, neighbor to neighbor. Tommy closed his eyes. He had no need for the printed music. He wasn't sure his feet were even touching the stage anymore. He was floating on high, back amongst his beloved rooftops, playing as he had never played before, pouring out all the beauty that had lain dormant in his heart and all the sweetness that was in his nature.

As Tommy sat down, he managed a glance at his mother. From the look on her face, she had forgotten her troubles, lost them in his music. Betsy sat transfixed, transported from this time to another, eyes closed tightly as though only her eyelids could hold back the flood of her emotions.

Suddenly, with a fanfare of disagreeable chords, the breezes encountered the evil that had been the town. Cymbals clashed, kettle drums rolled, and the audience squirmed nervously. The listeners were taken into a strange, lonely world, where man sat apart from man and no hands touched. It was a world of meanness and avarice, neighbor hating neighbor, wives shouting at husbands and husbands at wives, a place where no one could trust another.

Mr. Maki, the real estate salesman, held his knees

tightly, as though frightened at finding himself so suddenly alone. He looked over at his wife, who was holding a chicken drumstick in front of her like a weapon. "That's us!" he whispered. "That's us, Emmy, when we fight! Stupid and pigheaded. Trying to hurt each other! I was wrong this afternoon, Emmy! I don't want one more minute to go by without apologizing!"

Drums thundered and trombones blared as a great sixteen-horse freight wagon rumbled down the rocky road, its driver cursing and pounding the rumps of his sweaty horses. Trumpets made the little box buggy in its path squeal like a cornered hare, and clarinets shrieked the sound of temper shouting at temper.

Resting between passages, Tommy stole a glance at the audience, looking out to where the guttering lights barely held back the darkness. He saw John Branch standing out there alone, hands in his pockets. There was a sadness about the man. No one looked his way. No one offered him a seat on a blanket, a piece of chicken, or even a smile of recognition. He had given the park to the townspeople, but he had generated so much ill will in the past that he was still rendered invisible.

"At least he came here," Tommy thought. "Maybe not for my music. Maybe only to see how pretty his daughter looks in her black dress. But he came! Maybe, right now, that means a lot to Betsy."

It was the flutes' turn again. The spring breeze was trying to stay pure through the pall of chimney smoke and the belch of soot from factory smokestacks. Gray lines of tension were hanging over the town's nervous, oppressed citizens.

The first violinist glanced at Tommy over a stabbing sea of bows, smiling as though pleased to be a part of the evening. The audience sat riveted. No one coughed, shifted, straightened a leg, sighed, snored, dipped into a picnic basket, or tapped a restless toe.

Time ticked away like a runaway metronome. Stealing a glance at his pocket watch, Tommy was amazed that the concert was already half over. The second movement had vanished into the night air of history. Then the third was gone. Each had been more turbulent than the one before, and the Maestro's brow was shiny with perspiration, his hair wild as the mane of a white mustang.

Each man and woman in the audience seemed to have recognized his or her own miserable past in the music. The whole town was remorsefully standing trial, like prisoners certain of their conviction.

But the final movement brought hope. Brassy, blaring discord dissolved before the sweetness of flute, clarinet, and horn. Tommy glanced at Professor Trombley for direction and saw a look he had never seen before. The old man was smiling triumphantly as though he was planning not only a fitting start for Tommy's career, but a perfect climax for his own.

Betsy was busy with her contraption. Her hand rested on the big black crank along the side, and she watched the Professor as if for guidance. She looked as alert as a solo performer about to perform.

Good was now triumphing over evil! Fresh, pure breezes were sweeping out the town. The flutes were as lighthearted as fairies dancing in a meadow. The trumpets and trombones were as mellow and merry as

Sunday afternoon waltzes in the park. And the French horns were helping the audience recall their own most innocent dreams.

As Elaine took over on her flute to let Tommy rest, the boy looked again over the crowd. Moose, the constable, was there, looking strangely ordinary with two children on his lap. People were tapping their toes, smiling, touching. More than touching, they were holding hands. They were passing the chicken and sharing the lemonade, stranger reaching out to stranger, being truly nice to one another.

"This," Tommy thought, "is the way things should always be."

The Professor looked suddenly at Betsy and smiled. She rose to her feet, turned the crank on the telephone, lifted the earpiece, then spoke directly into the device.

Raising his arms, the old man brought the music to a crescendo. Then, suddenly, it was as if the whole world had stopped. Tommy glanced up from his music in surprise. "What is the old man doing?" he wondered.

Arms raised on high, the Maestro held the silence. He closed his eyes, as though waiting for a message from God before he resumed.

"Go!" shouted Betsy into the telephone.

Bong! Bong! Bong! went the Episcopal bells, shattering the silence.

Bong! Bong! Bong! went the Catholic bells, ringing sweet and pure.

Bong! Bong! Bong! went the Presbyterian bell down by the lake.

Bong! Bong! Bong! went the Methodists, just a tiny bit late as usual.

Tinkle! Tinkle! Tinkle! went the Lutherans, perfectly in tune.

Betsy looked over at Tommy in triumph. *Bong! Bong! Bong! Bong! Tinkle!* pealed all the church bells together. Professor Trombley moved his arms at last, and suddenly the full orchestra began playing along with the bells in one wild, stirring anthem of joy.

Gradually, Tommy became aware of a new sound— soft at first, then louder and louder until it mingled its thunder with the music. Applause! The audience members were on their feet, stomping, out of control, shouting for the composer, hugging each other in their excitement.

Professor Trombley looked stunned, but he struggled desperately to keep his orchestra playing. The symphony wasn't over yet! Where had manners gone? Not since he conducted Jenny Lind had he seen an audience get so carried away with emotion.

Vainly, the orchestra struggled on, trying to ignore the chaos. First the tuba went off on its own, then the trombones and the lead clarinet hit wild notes and dissolved in laughter. Suddenly the trumpet section rose up as a man, marching down the steps of the stage and through the crowd, playing a John Philip Sousa march.

Caught up in the welling of joy and good feeling, the crowd danced in behind, following the trumpets.

By now, Tommy and Betsy were holding hands, trying to shout words to each other. They might have stayed there forever, but the crowd swept them both up, along with John Branch and the Professor, and went marching across the park with them. John Branch looked for a moment as though he thought the crowd was going to hang him. Then he seemed to relax and looked at Betsy and Tommy with a proud smile. When Tommy last glimpsed the stage, he saw Elaine Rose, still playing away on her flute, determined to ignore what was happening.

Marching around the park on the shoulders of the crowd and holding hands with Betsy beside him, Tommy looked at the distant rooftops that had once been his only refuge. He knew, suddenly, that the roofs would always be there for him, but now he had a new life. He might climb again to the chimneys with his brushes, but he was a part of the town at last.